WARREN & Dragon

Scary
Sleepover

by Ariel Bernstein

illustrated by Mike Malbrough

VIKING

VIKING

An imprint of Penguin Random House LLC
New York

First published in the United States of America by Viking,
an imprint of Penguin Random House LLC, 2019

Text copyright © 2019 by Ariel Bernstein
Illustrations copyright © 2019 by Mike Malbrough

Visit us online at penguinrandomhouse.com

LIBRARY OF CONGRESS CATALOGING-IN-PUBLICATION DATA IS AVAILABLE.
ISBN 9780451481054

Printed in Canada

1   3   5   7   9   10   8   6   4   2

✹ ✹ ✹

For Mike Malbrough. —A.B.

For Abe. The best sleepover buddy. —M.M.

✹ ✹ ✹

CONTENTS

1

Outrageous Words

Some people might think that having a dragon for a pet is scary. I guess it sounds like it might be scary, because of the fire breathing and all, but I have a dragon for a pet and most of the time it's pretty normal. Except when Dragon does his weird little dancing jig. That's always terrifying.

But no one else even realizes he's my pet. They look at him and just see a stuffed animal. They can't hear him talk or see him move. This might sound weird, but I like that I don't have to share him with anyone. And I don't have to explain to anyone why having a dragon for a pet isn't scary.

Because when you're a seven-year-old kid in second grade, there's plenty of other stuff to be scared about. Like realizing you didn't do your homework ten minutes before you're supposed to leave for school. Even scarier than that? When your dad realizes you didn't do your homework ten minutes before you're supposed to leave for school.

"Argh!" my dad groans, looking at my incomplete vocabulary sheet. "Warren, you said you'd work on this after dinner last night."

I did tell my dad I'd work on the vocabulary sheet after dinner. But then Dragon and I started a contest over who could think up the most outrageous new word. Extra points for thinking up what the word means. It took an hour until I won with "flubbergitzooper." I decided it means coughing up goo while you're at the zoo. So in a way, I did work on vocabulary.

"It's not Warren's fault," my twin sister, Ellie, says. I look at her, surprised she's taking my side. "He's so irresponsible, Dad," she adds. "You can never believe he'll do anything he says."

I frown at Ellie. I don't want her to take my side anymore.

Dad hands me a pencil and points to the vocabulary sheet on the kitchen table. "Finish this," he says. "Now."

"Fine," I grumble. I take the vocabulary sheet and start working on it. I feel a breath of air over my shoulder and notice Dragon standing over me, looking at my writing. "I gotta finish this," I tell him, and turn back to the sheet. "Don't distract me again with any more weird word contests."

"I want a rematch," Dragon insists. "You only won because I was getting hungry and I can't think properly on an empty stomach. Sneeberleeber. It means a snail race. A slow one."

"Not now," I say, glancing through the kitchen doorway at my dad. He's helping Ellie reach for her jacket in the hallway closet.

"I can barely read your handwriting," Dragon says, and tsks. "Is that an *A* or a *P*?"

I look to where his claw is pointing. "That's a *U*," I say.

Dragon grimaces. "Your handwriting is scary. Also, wrotbloog. Wait, that's not outrageous enough. Wrotblooging."

"I'm not playing the outrageous word game now," I tell him. I quickly finish the vocabulary sheet. It's not perfect—it's not even good—but it's finished.

"Okay, but then you forfeit," Dragon announces, and crosses his arms.

I push the vocabulary sheet into my backpack and grab the jacket that Dad is holding out in his hands for me.

"You finished?" Dad asks.

"Easy as . . ." I pointedly look back toward Dragon and shout, "a habawablwa!" I rush through the front door before Dragon can think up another word. I zip up my jacket and pull on the gloves I had stuffed into the pockets. It's cold out, with snow still on the ground from a recent snowfall, but the path to school is clear where people shoveled.

Ellie runs ahead of Dad to catch up to me. "What's a habawablwa . . . ?"

"I haven't figured it out yet," I tell her.

Ellie shakes her head. "I don't know why I ask."

I shrug my shoulders. "I don't know why you ask either."

Ellie sighs and runs ahead of me. I stop and turn around to see where our dad is, immediately bumping into something.

An Invite

"Chitchimoo! It means I win!" Dragon yells into my face. I gasp and jump backward. I accidentally step into a mound of snow. "Ha!" he says, and does his little jig. "I win! Chitchimoo for the win!"

"Please stop dancing," I moan with my hands over my eyes. I stomp my shoe against the sidewalk to bang the snow off.

"Not only did I win the outrageous word contest, but I also scared you," Dragon proclaims with a huge grin.

"The only thing you scared me with was your dancing," I argue.

Dragon raises an eyebrow. "I totally scared you. You jumped backward and everything."

"I was not scared!" I shout. Dragon looks like he doesn't believe me at all.

"It's okay to admit you get scared sometimes," Dragon tells me. "For example, I am petrified when I open the cupboards in the kitchen and find only two bags of marshmallows left. Those might not even last me a full day. I also get scared at bathtime. My wings get all wrinkly when I'm wet. Plus, you know how I feel about teddy bears."

I nod my head. "I know, I know. You think teddy bears go around stealing s'mores."

Dragon shudders. "They're terrifying creatures."

"Hey, Warren!" someone calls. My friend Michael, who is also my next-door neighbor, is running to catch up with me. My dad is walking next to Michael's mom Paula, and Paula is holding the hand of Michael's little sister, Addie.

"Hi, Michael," Dragon and I say at the same time.

Michael looks a little flushed from running, but his eyes are wide with excitement about something. "Guess what?" he announces.

"I've been elected mayor?" Dragon guesses. I give him a glance. "What?" he says. "It could happen."

"What's going on?" I ask Michael.

"Remember how my moms got me a camping tent for Christmas but I thought I'd have to wait a couple of months until spring to use it?" I nod my head. "Well, they said I can set it up in the basement this weekend and have a sleepover!"

"That's cool," I say.

"So you want to come?" Michael asks.

"To where?"

Michael snorts. "To the sleepover on Friday!"

"A sleepover?" I repeat, thinking about it. I've never been to a sleepover before. But if it's with Michael, it should be fun.

"Sure," I say.

"Great!" Michael replies.

"I can't wait for the sleepover," Dragon muses. "There'll probably be pizza, and treats, and games." It does sound pretty great. Dragon continues, "Also, because we'll be in a different house at nighttime, there might be strange noises, dark hallways, and possibly monsters all around just waiting for new victims to terrorize. Should be interesting."

Strange noises? Dark hallways? Monsters?

"Kaplomsky," I say. It's a word I just made up. It means I'm confused.

3

What Are You Scared Of?

As we near school, Dragon turns back toward our house. He shouts "barummalot" on his way.

Michael and I walk into the building together. He's really excited about the sleepover, as it'll be his first one, too. He talks about games we'll play and food we'll eat. It all sounds fun until Michael tells me his older brother, Jayden, explained that the best part of sleepovers is telling scary stories before bedtime.

"Jayden told me a whole bunch of really creepy stories he learned from overnight camp," Michael says happily.

"You don't get scared from the stories?" I ask.

"Nah," Michael replies, and waves his hand. "They're all just made up. And it's fun to get a little scared. Don't you think?"

I try to smile in agreement but I think it comes out like a grimace. Luckily, Michael doesn't seem to notice when we part at the front doors. Michael goes to the first grade class-rooms while I walk over to my second grade classroom. About half my class is already there, some in their seats and some playing around.

My desk is near the back and next to Alison Cohen's desk. She's sitting quietly, reading a book just like she always does before the school bell rings.

I put my jacket and book bag in my cubby before taking out a notebook and pencil. I bring them over to my desk and sit down.

"Hey, Alison," I say.

"Hi, Warren," she says politely, but doesn't look up from her book.

I'm still thinking about the sleepover, and I

am starting to get worried. When I look at Alison, she doesn't seem like she has anything to be scared of. I know it'll be a couple of minutes before our teacher, Mrs. Tierney, starts the class, so I decide to see if I'm right.

"Alison, can I ask you a question?"

Alison stops reading and glances at me with both eyebrows raised. I can see she looks suspicious. It may be because I once asked her at lunch how many mini marshmallows she thought I could put up my nose before anyone noticed. I also once asked her which she thought would be worse, a dragon who burped fire or a dragon who

couldn't burp at all. And in the middle of music class, I might have asked Alison how loud she thought I'd have to sing to break a window.

Alison puts down her book and sighs. "What do you want to ask me?"

"What are you scared of?"

Alison raises her eyebrows again. "You really want to know what I'm afraid of?"

I nod.

"Wait," Alison says slowly. "You're not going to take my answer and then use it to scare me later, are you?" She's scrunched her face up so that she looks super serious.

"I wouldn't do that," I say. I do not say that's actually an interesting idea.

"Okay," Alison replies, and seems to relax. She puts her finger to her cheek like she's thinking hard. But she doesn't get to answer before our teacher, Mrs. Tierney, calls the class to attention. We stand for the pledge of allegiance and then sit again while the morning announcements are read over the loudspeaker.

"So what are you scared of?" I whisper to Alison.

Alison looks pointedly at Mrs. Tierney and then back at me. "I'm scared we're gonna get in trouble for talking during announcements," she whispers back.

"Yeah, but what else?"

Alison looks straight ahead like she's ignoring me.

I try listening to the morning announcements but they're too boring. I turn back to Alison.

"Are you afraid of heights? Scary movies?" Alison's still ignoring me so I start to doodle scary animals like sharks and lions on my notebook to show her. "Terrifying animals?"

"I *love* animals," Alison replies, looking at me with a glare. "*All* animals."

Given that Alison's home is filled with pets, I believe her.

"What about being someplace you haven't been before? Like at night?" I ask, as quietly as

I can. "Even if you're there with a friend, it's still dark and you don't know what spooky things are there. And maybe it's where people tell scary stories."

Alison thinks for a moment. "Like a sleepover?"

"Uh, I guess you could call it that," I reply, surprised she guessed right away what I was talking about.

"Oh, definitely." Alison nods her head in understanding. She seems to have forgotten to ignore me. "I always get scared at sleepovers."

"You do?"

"I've been on three, and each time I've gotten too scared to stay the whole night so my parents have had to come pick me up."

"All right, class," Mrs. Tierney says. The announcements must have finished. "Let's start on our writing workshop."

Everyone turns their notebook to their writing pages. I write down, "Why do you keep going on sleepovers if you're scared?" and show it to Alison.

Alison shrugs. "The only way I'll get over my fear is to face it," she tells me in a low voice. "At least, that's what my parents say. And I always have a good time at the sleepovers until it's time to tell scary stories. Then I can never fall asleep and have to go home."

I try to imagine what it'd be like to be in a sleeping bag in the tent in the basement of Michael's house. Michael would probably fall asleep easily since he'd be at his own house. Dragon would probably be in a food coma from eating all the great food Michael's moms always have. I'd be lying awake, listening for any odd noises. Suddenly I'd hear some creaking and hissing. I'd nudge Michael and Dragon, but they wouldn't notice me. The noises would come closer. Closer.

I gasp. Mrs. Tierney looks over and raises an eyebrow. Alison waits until she's turned away before saying, "What's wrong?"

"Is it really embarrassing to have your parents come pick you up at a sleepover?" I ask.

I can't imagine waking Michael up to tell him I need to go home because I hear scary noises. Michael's a good friend, but I'm a year older than him. I don't want him to think I'm a scaredy-cat.

"It is kind of embarrassing," Alison admits. "I try to hold out as long as I can, but I'm never able to fall asleep. I still say yes whenever I'm invited to a sleepover."

"Right, to face your fear," I say.

"It's also because if I say no, I worry I won't get asked on another one. I haven't been invited to a sleepover in a while. I think I'm ready to stay the whole night now, but I haven't had the chance lately to try." Alison looks a little sad when she says that.

"Alison? Warren?" Mrs. Tierney calls out from her desk. I see that Alison's face has turned red. "Are you working on your writing?"

"Yeah, it's about facing fears and stuff," I reply. Mrs. Tierney looks surprised but nods her head like we should continue writing.

I realize that Alison's a lot more honest about how she feels about sleepovers than I am. I'm not comfortable telling her how I feel, so I just write, "Maybe you'll get the chance again soon," and nudge her elbow to look. She writes back, "I hope so."

4

The Sleepover Deal

Even after talking with Alison, I'm not sure I want to face my fears by going on the sleepover. I wonder if I could somehow get out of it without admitting I'm too scared to go.

I think about it all afternoon after school, until I finally have an idea right before dinner.

"Tacos are ready!" my dad calls out from the kitchen.

"I hope he remembered the jalapeños this time," Dragon says, scurrying out of my bedroom to head toward, the kitchen. I follow behind.

My parents and Ellie fill up their plates with taco shells, ground meat, shredded cheese, lettuce, and salsa.

Dragon searches the fixings. "No jalapeños," he moans. He dips a claw into the salsa and licks it. "Proofroonunu. That means that this salsa is way too mild." He looks around the table accusingly. "It's like you people haven't lived with a dragon for seven years. Sheesh."

I slowly start to make my taco with extra cheese, waiting for an opening.

"So how was school today?" Mom asks. I smile, knowing this is my chance.

"Michael got a tent for Christmas," I say casually.

"Oh, that's interesting," Mom replies, even though I know it's not that interesting. "It's too cold to go camping now though."

"He wants to set it up in his basement," I tell her. "And he wants me to come over for a sleepover in the tent on Friday."

"That sounds like fun!" Dad says.

"Sleepovers are the *best!*" Ellie agrees. El-lie's already been on a bunch of sleepovers at her friends' houses. And I know she must not have gotten scared because she's never called my parents to come pick her up.

"Yeah, it should be fun," I say carefully. "Al-though I think I heard that the tent may not be made well and it may collapse suddenly. But we probably won't get hurt too badly." My parents glance at each other.

"Michael said the tent isn't working?" Mom asks.

I take a bite of my taco so I don't have to answer.

"Well, we can always go and help set it up," Dad offers.

I swallow my bite. "I think it sets up fine, but then collapses later. Like, when we'll be sleeping." I'm hoping that my parents will decide to call off the sleepover if they imagine my mangled body caused by a falling tent.

"I call Michael's beanbag chair to sleep in," Dragon whispers to me.

"If you're not comfortable sleeping in a tent, Warren, you can ask Michael's moms if you can have a sleepover in Michael's bedroom instead," Mom suggests. "We have an extra sleeping bag you can bring. Or you can sleep in the basement in sleeping bags without the tent."

I hadn't thought of those alternatives. I have to think of something else, fast.

"But won't you miss me?" I say.

Mom and Dad glance at each other again.

"Of course, Warren," Mom begins. "But it's just for one night."

"You have to go on the sleepover!" Ellie suddenly says. We all look at her. "What? I've never had the house to myself before."

"Mom and I would still be here, Ellie," Dad points out.

"Yeah, but he'd be gone," Ellie says, and waves at me. "I've never had a night in this house without Warren here."

"Me either," Dragon adds, raising his arm.

"What are you going to do on Friday night that you can't do with me home?" I ask.

Ellie smiles. "Host my own sleepover," she replies like it's obvious.

"You can have a sleepover with me here," I say.

Ellie rolls her eyes. "The point of a sleepover is to have fun with your friends. You'd probably throw water on us in the middle of the night and claim it was because your dragon doll started a fire and you needed to put it out."

Dragon giggles. "That'd be so funny. Wait, did she call me a doll again?"

I cross my arms. "I would not do that. Fires aren't funny."

"Fine. Then you'd hide all the good snacks so we couldn't raid the cupboards after Mom and Dad fall asleep."

"Ellie!" Mom says.

I don't say anything, because I probably would do that.

"I want to invite Carly, Madeline, and maybe one other friend," Ellie says.

I suddenly remember something. "You should invite Alison," I tell her.

Ellie looks at me with surprise. "Alison?" she asks. Ellie and Alison are friendly, but I know they aren't close friends. "Why her?"

"Um . . ." I try to think up a good reason that doesn't involve me admitting I'm being too nice or sappy. "Alison is kind of goody-goody and she probably won't let you leave slime under my bed covers or anything like that."

Ellie shrugs like she accepts my explanation.

"If you invite Alison, I'll go on the sleepover at Michael's," I offer.

"Deal," Ellie immediately agrees. She reaches her hand out and we shake on it.

"When did we agree to have three of Ellie's friends over Friday night?" Dad whispers to Mom.

Mom shakes her head. "I guess I'll need to get more snacks for the cupboard raiding."

5

Telling Dragon

Dragon and I decide to make a snow fort in the backyard after dinner before it gets too dark out. Instead of working on the fort, I end up pacing. I can't stop imagining that I'll get scared at the sleepover and have to tell Michael I need to go home.

"What is wrong with you?" Dragon asks.

"Nothing's wrong with me."

"Are you upset because of what I did to your laundry hamper?"

I stop pacing. "What did you do to my laundry hamper?"

Dragon looks up and whistles. "It doesn't matter. But there *is* something wrong with you," he insists. "You only ate one taco at dinner. That's just weird. Even with no jalapeños, you should have been eating at least four."

I wonder if telling Dragon what's bothering me will help me feel better like it did when I told Alison.

"If I tell you something, you promise you won't laugh at me?"

"I pinky promise I won't laugh at you," Dragon says solemnly, and holds up his outermost claw. I reach over the snow fort to take it with my pinky finger. We shake.

"Okay," I begin. "I'm nervous about going to the sleepover Friday at Michael's."

"Why?" Dragon asks in surprise. "Wait, is it because you're worried they won't have sleep covers for my wings? Because I was worried about that, too, and I'm planning on packing my extra pair."

"No. I'm worried I'll get too scared at night and want to come back home."

Dragon looks at me for a moment before letting out a giggle.

"You said you wouldn't laugh at me!" I exclaim. I wonder if Michael would react the same way if he found out.

Dragon crouches down behind the fort so I can't see his face. I hear him take a couple of deep breaths before poking his head back up.

"I didn't laugh at you," Dragon says, covering his mouth with his claw. I can tell he's trying to stifle another giggle. "I laughed *near* you."

I glare at him before crunching some snow

together in my hand and aiming for Dragon's belly.

Dragon jumps out of the way just in time. "Aw, don't be like that," he says. I throw another snowball at him and he ducks down but it grazes his shoulder. He smiles at me mischievously and before long we're tossing snowballs back and forth. By the time we're both laid out on the ground on our backs and out of breath, I've got snow on top of my hat, under my jacket collar, and in my boots. I've never felt better.

"Dimpshompalong," Dragon says. "That means we should have a snowball fight again in an hour or so."

"Okay, but don't make fun of me again," I tell him.

Dragon sighs. "I was just surprised you're worried because of a sleepover, Warren. I mean, you live with the most fearsome creature of all time. You're not scared of *me*."

I push myself slightly up on my elbows and look over at Dragon. I raise an eyebrow.

"Dragons are very, very fierce!" he insists. Dragon suddenly seems to remember he's wearing a puffy unicorn hat with attached scarf. He touches them gingerly and grins. "Well, sometimes we can be." He hops up. "Look, I know exactly how you can prepare for the sleepover."

"I know. I know," I interrupt, and force myself to fully stand as well. "I have to face my fears on Friday by going to the sleepover and just trying to deal with it." I brush snow off the front of my jacket.

Dragon waves his claws around. "No, no, no. You have to prepare way before then. We'll go over to Michael's house and check it for scary stuff before the sleepover. If we don't find anything suspicious, you know you'll be safe Friday night."

"And if we do find something suspicious?"

"We confront it and . . ."

"And?"

"And?"

Dragon taps a claw against his snout like he's thinking hard. "And we'll see how it goes."

"That doesn't sound like a good plan."

"Yeah, but it's the best one we've got," Dragon points out. He flexes his muscles. "Besides, is anything really going to mess with a dragon? Let's go."

"Now?" I ask.

Dragon gets behind me to push me in the direction of Michael's house. "Don't worry. I'll be right behind you the whole time."

6

The First Plan

Michael's mom Paula opens the front door. "Hi, Warren!" she says with a smile. "You look cold. Come on in."

"Thanks," I say, and walk in with Dragon next to me.

"What a well-dressed dragon doll," Paula adds.

I look at Dragon. I can tell he's having trouble deciding between being mad he was called a doll or pleased at the compliment. Dragon touches his scarf and hat and flutters his eyelashes at Paula. The compliment has won out.

I take off my snow-covered boots. Dragon

shakes himself a little so that snow falls off him
and onto the welcome mat.

"Do your parents know you're here?" Paula
asks.

"Oops," I say, realizing I forgot to tell anyone.

"It's okay. I'll call them now. Michael's upstairs in his room. He's excited about the
sleepover Friday!"

"Uh, me too." I start to head toward the stairs
when Dragon taps me on the shoulder.

"You go to Michael's room and check everything on the way," he whispers. "I'm going to

check the downstairs for anything scary that could pop out at us in the middle of the night."

I nod and make my way to Michael's room. Everything I pass looks pretty normal and not scary. The hallway walls are painted a light yellow, the carpeting on the stairs is its usual blue, and the framed pictures on the walls are all of Michael's family. I pause to look at the photos to see if any of the eyes move like they did when I went to a haunted house attraction the previous Halloween, but the eyeballs keep looking in the same direction.

I make a move like I'm about to walk away, and then turn my head quickly back to look at the photos again. No change in the eyeballs.

I finally get to Michael's room and knock on the door.

"Come in!" Michael shouts, and I open the door to find him on his bed reading a comic book. He looks surprised to see me but sits up and smiles. "Hey, Warren!"

"Hi, Michael." I try to look around his room

all casual like I'm not searching for anything terrifying that could crawl to the basement on Friday night and jump out at me. The toy soccer players on the floor aren't moving, the light fixtures aren't flickering, and the books on the bookshelf aren't jumping off the shelves. So far, everything checks out.

"I've been planning for the sleepover," Michael says proudly. "First, we're going to order pizza."

"Great," I say. I do not even have to force myself to sound excited. I like Michael's plans so far.

"Then, we're going to have our first dessert. Ice cream sundaes."

First dessert? That means there'll be more. I try to remember why I was scared of the sleepover.

"Next, we're going to play foosball and a game of checkers, and watch a TV show. Then it'll be time for the second dessert. A cookie topped with whipped creamed and sprinkles.

My moms don't know about the second dessert though, so we'll have to be quiet."

It seems to me that being quiet while getting the second dessert goes without saying, so I just nod my head again.

"Then . . ." Michael grins mischievously and rubs his hands together. "Come with me." Michael pushes off his bed and walks past me to the hallway. I follow behind.

We head down two flights of stairs until we reach the basement.

"This is where the tent will go." Michael motions to one side of the room. "I figure we should wait to tell scary stories right before bedtime. The later at night, the better!"

"Um . . . I don't think I know any scary stories," I say. I do not say I do not even want to think of any scary stories before bedtime.

Michael waves his hand like it's not a problem. "You can just make some up. It'll be easy to think of some once all the lights are off and you hear the creepy basement noises."

"Basement noises?" I look around the room, trying to see where noises would come from.

"At night there's lots of noises down here," Michael explains. For some reason he doesn't seem bothered by this. "And with the lights off, it's extra spooky. Cool, huh? I mean, Addie gets scared of the noises at night. But she's just a little kid."

"Yeah," I say like I understand. I do not say that Michael's little sister, Addie, might have the right idea. After all, I do not want Michael to compare me to his three-year-old sister.

I suddenly hear a thud coming from near the window above. "What's that?"

Michael looks to the window and shrugs. "I don't know. Maybe an icicle falling?"

"Oh, that makes sense." I feel silly for getting worried.

"But if this was Friday night and we were telling stories, I'd probably say it was Bigfoot trying to find an opening to the house." Michael scrunches his face like he's thinking of something. "Or maybe an escaped convict."

I hear a thud again and jump.

"Uh, I should probably get going home, Michael," I say, trying not to gulp.

"Oh, okay," Michael replies. I can tell he's disappointed that I'm leaving so early but I figure it's a plus that I'm not running out. I don't want Michael to get suspicious and figure out what my problem is.

We make our way upstairs. Addie comes out of the kitchen, dragging Dragon by his tail in one hand with a half-eaten chocolate chip cookie in the other. Addie is also wearing Dragon's unicorn scarf and hat. Dragon sees me and Michael and wiggles out of Addie's grasp.

"I was minding my own business, checking the chips bags, the cereal boxes, and the cookie jar for anything suspicious. I was in the middle of seeing whether the cookies were poisoned by evil kitchen spirits, when she grabbed me!" Dragon points at Addie and glares. "She took my scarf and hat, and the rest of my cookie! She's a blableebloohacker! Blableebloohackers are even scarier than teddy bears!"

"Can I please keep Mister Dragoo?" Addie asks me. "We wanna play more dress-up and have a tickle contest."

"I did *not* agree to that!" Dragon exclaims.

He jumps away to hide behind me. "Quick! Let's make our escape! She can keep the scarf and hat."

"Maybe another time, Addie," I tell her.

Addie pouts.

"Aw, she is kinda cute," Dragon says, peering at Addie over my shoulder. "Still, she took my cookie. That's unforgiveable."

I put my boots and coat on before saying bye to Michael and Addie.

"I don't think we accomplished anything," I tell Dragon on our walk back home.

"That's not true," Dragon replies. "Now we know the cookies aren't poisoned."

7

Late Night Research

Later that night, I can't fall asleep. Turns out, if I can't sleep, Dragon can't fall asleep either.

"Stop tossing and turning," Dragon says. "You're keeping me awake. I'm so tired I can't even think of an outrageous word that means you're keeping me awake."

"Sorry," I reply.

I try to stay still. I listen for loud noises like I heard in Michael's basement. The wind outside is rattling tree branches, but it doesn't seem scary at all from my bed. I sigh. Michael is going to think I'm such a baby if I get scared at his house because of something like wind rattling.

"Stop sighing."

"I can't fall asleep, Dragon."

Now Dragon sighs. "So our first plan to take care of Friday night didn't work."

"It did not."

"It's okay. I've already got another plan."

I sigh and turn on my lamp.

"Stop sighing! This is a great plan. Guaranteed to work." Dragon must take my silence for acceptance because he continues. "What we need to do is find a lot of scary stuff, face *those* fears, and then by the time you have the sleepover it won't seem as scary compared to all the other scary stuff you faced."

I'm confused and it must show, because Dragon tries to explain again. "What if you went into a room full of anacondas with laser eyes? That'd be pretty terrifying, right?"

"Yeah."

"So after you faced a room full of anacondas with laser eyes, a little tiny sleepover won't seem very scary in comparison."

"In case you haven't noticed, there aren't any anacondas with laser eyes nearby," I say, and motion around my bedroom.

"No, but there are plenty of *other* scary things in Eddington, New Jersey." Dragon then grins the widest grin I've ever seen and taps his claws together. "It's time for some research," he declares, and motions for me to follow him. "Come on. We're not getting any sleep tonight anyway."

I follow Dragon with light steps to my dad's home office. He sits by the computer keyboard and hands me a pad of paper and a pen. "Take some notes." Dragon turns on the computer and starts typing. "Scary . . . stuff . . . in . . . boring . . . suburbs. Okay, here we go."

I get ready to write down what he finds.

"Number one. Jumping off roofs."

I stop writing after "jumping." "That's not scary," I argue. "That's just dumb."

"Even when there's snow on the ground to fall onto?" Dragon asks.

"Still dumb."

Dragon huffs and continues to tap. "Fine. Here's a good one. Confronting a rabid squirrel."

"That's also more dumb than scary."

Dragon takes the pad and pen from me and starts writing a list by himself. He won't let me see what he's writing.

When he's finished, Dragon hides the pad of paper behind him. "Part of being scared is the element of surprise," he says. "Tomorrow, after school, we're going to start facing your fears. Even if they're dumb. It's for your own good.

Plincherstoo. It means you can't live your life being afraid of things."

❌   ❌   ❌

I start school the next day being scared again. Except I'm not scared of the sleepover. I'm scared of Dragon's list of fears for me to confront later that afternoon. I'm getting really tired of being scared of stuff.

Alison sits down next to me with a big smile. "Hey, Warren!" she says.

"Hi."

"I'm so excited for the sleepover!" Alison clasps her hands together.

I had forgotten Ellie promised to invite her. "You'll have fun," I tell her. "Are you nervous you'll want to leave early?"

Alison takes a strand of her curly hair and pulls on it as she considers my question. "I am a *little* nervous it'll happen again. But I've got to try. I like Ellie and her friends, and this way I'll get to know them better."

"Just make sure you guys don't go into my room to pull any pranks."

"You won't be there?" Alison asks.

"I'll be at Michael's next door for our own sleepover. It's my first sleepover."

"Oh, fun!"

We're quiet for a couple of moments until Alison glances at me again. "Are *you* worried about getting scared and having to leave early?"

"No!" I say, way too quickly. Alison raises her eyebrows. "I mean, definitely not. Maybe not." Alison doesn't look like she's going to laugh at me like Dragon did. Maybe because she told me about how she got scared, I feel like I can tell her the truth. "There's a possibility I'll get scared. I've never been on a sleepover before, so I really don't know."

Alison nods her head like she understands. "Since you'll be just next door, maybe we can come up with some sort of system to help if one of us is getting scared and wants to go home. Like, if you're having trouble, you can shine a flashlight on and off three times at Ellie's window, and I'll come meet you outside to talk. As long as I haven't fallen asleep already. But I'm a light sleeper."

"Really?" I ask. "You'd do that?"

"Sure," Alison replies. "I mean, we're friends. Right?"

I hadn't really thought about being friends with Alison before. I like talking with Alison. And I like hanging out with her sometimes.

"Right," I say. "And you can shine a flashlight at the basement window in Michael's house if you're having trouble. Then I'll come meet you."

Alison smiles. "It's a plan!"

I smile back. It's a better plan than any that Dragon's come up with. I stop smiling when I remember Dragon still has his own plan for after school.

8

The Second Plan

I walk into my house slowly. I don't know what Dragon's prepared for the afternoon so I'm trying to be cautious.

Ellie rushes past me and Dad into the kitchen. "I've got to eat a snack quickly," she announces. "I have so much planning to do for the sleepover."

"*After* your homework," Dad replies.

Ellie grimaces but nods her head.

I'm about to join Ellie at the table for snacks when my arm is grabbed from behind.

"You don't have time for snacks," Dragon says as I whirl around.

"You scared me!" I say, and pull my arm out of Dragon's grasp. "What do you mean there's no time for snacks? There's *always* time for snacks."

"It's taken care of," Dragon replies, and wiggles his eyebrows mysteriously.

"What about homework?" I say. I do not say I can't believe I'm actually mentioning homework like I want to do it or something just to put off Dragon's "plan."

"Also taken care of."

"What does that mean?"

Dragon curls a claw toward himself as though I should follow him. I look longingly at the crackers and cheese and chocolate milk that Ellie's set out for herself, hoping that there will still be some later.

I follow Dragon, and he leads me downstairs to our basement. I look around, but I don't see anything different or scary. Then Dragon turns to go back up the stairs.

"Why'd we come down here just to leave?" I ask.

"Shhhh," Dragon replies, putting a claw to his snout.

Next I follow him to my dad's office room. Again, I see nothing different. After that we head up to the attic. There's a bunch of dust on cardboard boxes and a few spiderwebs near the corners, but nothing frightening.

"What . . ." I begin. But Dragon has already begun walking down the attic ladder. I roll my eyes and follow him down. I wonder if Dragon is trying to make me scared of running out of breath?

Eventually Dragon makes his way to the backyard. When he comes to the edge of our property line, Dragon whirls around.

"Are you confused?" he asks.

"Yes."

"Are you cold?"

"I'm standing in the middle of snow without a coat or gloves. Of course I'm cold."

"Are you hungry?"

"*Yes.*"

Dragon spreads his claws out in the air and waves them around. "Are you . . . scared?"

"Not really."

Dragon looks disappointed. He reaches down to grab a bowl that's been left on the ground. I realize it's full of twigs and weird looking berries.

"Here's your snack," Dragon declares.

"I'm not eating that," I reply.

"Why? Are you . . . *scared*?" Dragon asks with his eyebrows raised.

I look at the bowl. "Am I scared to eat that? Yes, I am terrified to eat that. Rishooey. That means any normal person would be scared to eat a bowl of twigs and strange berries."

"Ha!" Dragon says, and jumps up and down. "The first part of my plan is a success! Now, on to the next."

Dragon begins marching back toward the

house, leaving me behind as I sputter.

"What?" I shout. "*This* is your plan? To make me walk all over the house for nothing and then give me twigs to eat?"

"It's only the first part," Dragon calls back to me. "Take a few moments to compose yourself, and then you'll find out what the next part of my plan is!"

I trudge through the snow back to the house. I don't see Dragon and decide I'm going to need to eat a real snack before dealing with the second part of his plan.

I open the cupboards to look for the crackers and realize . . . they're gone.

"Ellie!" I shout. "Did you finish all the crackers?"

I hear Ellie's bedroom door open. "No!" she yells down. "Quit bugging me!" Then she shuts her door loudly.

That's weird. I don't see the crackers anywhere. I figure I'll eat some cookies instead.

Except when I start to look for the cookies, I don't see them either. I don't see the marshmallows, the chips, or the pretzels. I don't even see the healthy biscuits Mom and Dad eat. I hurry to open the fridge. The cheese is missing and so is the chocolate sauce for making chocolate milk.

"Getting scared?" I hear Dragon's voice behind me.

"I am getting very, very angry," I reply with my hands on my hips. "Where's all the food?"

"There are still some carrots in the fridge," Dragon says.

"That's not funny."

"Don't worry, you can earn back all the snacks. You just have to finish the third and final part of my plan."

I take a deep breath before pinching my nose. "What is the third and final part of your plan, Dragon?"

"Follow me to your bedroom."

As I walk behind Dragon, I hear my stomach rumble. This had better go fast.

Dragon steps aside at my bedroom door to let me go in. I walk in and at first don't understand what I'm looking at. There's white everywhere. And then I see it's pieces of white paper covering my bed and my desk, and all over my floor.

"What *is* this?" I say, picking up some pieces of paper. I realize they're ripped from a math workbook Mom had brought home one day thinking it'd help me learn subtraction. But I hid it under my mattress, so she eventually forgot about it.

"Homework," Dragon says like it's obvious.

"I only have two sheets of homework from school for today," I tell him. "I'm not doing all this extra work."

Dragon shrugs. "Then you won't earn back your snacks. You are now tired from walking all over the house, hungry from not having a snack, and annoyed at all this homework. Are you sufficiently scared now?"

I feel my mouth drop open, but am unable

to form a sentence. "You . . . what . . . crazy . . ."

"There's no need to thank me," Dragon says with a wave of his claw. "I know this is terrifying for you. But now anything you encounter at the sleepover, such as ghosts, a seven-foot-tall teddy bear, whatever, won't be as scary as this afternoon."

I set the papers back down on the floor and march over to Dragon to look him right in the eye.

"Dragon, you're not scaring me! You're driving me insane!"

"But doesn't it *scare* you that you're going insane?"

I sigh. I know Dragon means well, but I'm feeling a lot more angry and annoyed than scared.

"Dragon, you need to put the snacks back in the kitchen right now, or I'm not taking you to Michael's for the sleepover."

Dragon gasps and covers his snout with both claws. "You wouldn't!"

I look around the room at the papers. "Oh, I definitely would."

"But how are you going to prepare yourself in case you get scared at the sleepover?"

I step back, seeing that he has a point. "I guess I'll just have to go with the original plan."

"What's that?"

"I'm going on the sleepover, and I'm going to face my fears head on."

Dragon pats me on the shoulder. "That's not as good of a plan as my plan, but I support your foolhardy decision."

"Thanks. Now can you put the snacks back?"

"Um, sure. I can put back what's left at least." Dragon pulls a bag full of the snacks out from under my bed and hands me a small package. "I left the healthy biscuits for you."

9

Getting Ready

Friday after school, I pack for the sleepover. Dragon looks into my bag.

"You've got a toothbrush, pajamas, a flashlight, and a change of clothes," he says after rummaging around. "Where's everything else?"

"What else do I need?"

"Lots of stuff. Don't worry. I've got it covered."

I'm about to ask Dragon what he's talking about when I notice Ellie peeking her head into my bedroom.

"Oh, you're still here," she says.

"It's only four o'clock," I say, pointing to my wall clock.

Dragon reaches over me to take
the bag. "Teddy bear repellent,
wing sleep covers, rope for last-
minute escapes, netting to catch
goblins . . ." he mutters as he puts
stuff into the bag.

"Yeah, but you'll have such a great time,
you'll want start the sleepover as soon as pos-
sible." Ellie widens her eyes like she's trying to
look innocent. But I know her better than that.

"Why are you trying to get rid of me?" I
ask her.

Ellie widens her eyes even more, like she can't
believe what I'm saying. "I just want you
to have fun," she protests. "Plus, my
friends are going to be here soon and
I figure we'll get on your nerves so
you might as well go to Michael's
early." I raise an eyebrow at Ellie.

"Okay, I figure you'll get on *our* nerves so you might as well be at Michael's." She walks into my room and takes the bag from Dragon, peering into it. "*What* are you bringing?"

I grab the bag and zip it shut. "It's nothing important."

"Just make sure you have room in there to bring your dragon doll," Ellie says.

Dragon jumps up. "Did she seriously call *me* a doll! Again! Flumbasha. That means ridiculous! Come on, Warren. Let's go to Michael's where I'm appreciated."

I have to agree. There's not much to do at home, and Michael told me I could come over whenever. And it's still daylight, so the thought of starting the sleepover now doesn't seem scary at all.

"Okay, I'm going," I tell Ellie. "But stay out of my room."

Ellie rolls her eyes. "Why would we even want to go in your room?"

I'm about to answer with a list of all the great stuff I have hidden in my bedroom, like my collection of comic books, my stash of leftover candy canes from Christmas melted onto leftover candy bars from Halloween, plus the ninja training manual for worms Dragon and I wrote, but I realize that would defeat the purpose of convincing Ellie to stay away.

"You're right," I say. "There's just dirty socks everywhere." I add a shrug for effect.

"Ew," Ellie replies, scrunching her nose.

"See you later!" I call out. I see my dad taking out extra pillows for Ellie's friends from the linen closet. "I'm going to Michael's now." I tell him.

Dad looks up. "Have fun, Warren!"

"Thanks," I say, and walk down the stairs. Dragon's already at the front door, about to open it. "Wait for me," I tell him.

"Someone knocked," he informs me, and finishes opening the door. Alison is standing there holding a sleeping bag, with a large purple bag

over her shoulder. She turns and waves to a car parked on the street. It must be her parents, as they leave once she waves.

"I didn't want them to come inside and embarrass me," Alison explains.

"I understand," Dragon assures her, even

though Alison doesn't notice him. "Warren and his family embarrass me *all* the time."

"You can go inside," I say as I walk out the door. "Ellie's upstairs but her other friends aren't here yet. Make sure no one goes into my room, okay?"

"Okay," Alison promises. "I'm excited! Are you excited? I'm really hoping I don't get scared. I did a lot of jumping jacks after school so I'd get tired and can hopefully fall asleep easily."

"You did?" I wish I had thought of that plan. I'm wondering if I should do jumping jacks before going to Michael's.

"Yeah, but then I remembered everyone eats a lot of dessert at sleepovers so it'll be hard to fall asleep after a sugar rush. No matter how many jumping jacks I did."

"Oh." I don't want to give up eating dessert at Michael's.

"I brought my flashlight just in case though. Three flashes at the window, remember?"

I pat my bag. "Yeah, I remember. I have my flashlight."

Mom comes up behind Alison. "Hey, Alison!" she says. "Ellie will be so glad you're here." Then she looks at me. "Tell Michael and his family we say 'hi.' Have fun!"

Everyone assumes I'm going to have fun at Michael's. I guess I might as well try.

10

The Fun Part

Michael's already waiting for me at his front door when I arrive.

"I kept looking out the window to see when you were coming," he explains with a grin. "Put your jacket and boots in the closet. Then let's put your bag and dragon up in my room."

"That's thoughtful of Michael," Dragon whispers to me as we make our way to Michael's bedroom. "I could use a nap before the nightly shenanigans."

We leave my bag on Michael's floor and Dragon plops himself onto Michael's beanbag. We quickly head back downstairs to the kitchen.

Addie, Jayden, and both of Michael's moms greet me.

"We're just about to order pizza," Michael's mom Nia tells us. "I know Addie and Paula want plain, Michael wants pepperoni, and Jayden and I like mushroom pizza." Michael makes a face when she says "mushroom." "What would you like, Warren?"

I'm surprised she asks me. When my parents order pizza, they always just get a large pizza, half cheese for me and Ellie, and half peppers for my parents. "I guess I'll try the pepperoni too," I reply.

Michael smiles at me like I made the right choice. I smile back.

"We're gonna play foosball in the den now," Michael informs his moms. "Let us know when the pizza arrives."

Michael and I play foosball for a while and we have so much fun, we don't even keep track of who's winning. We start to play a game of checkers, but Addie wanders into the den and insists

that the checker pieces are meant for stacking, not playing. Jayden comes in and chuckles when he sees that Addie has taken over the game.

"Come on, Addie," he says, and leans down to pick her up. Addie squeals. "Pizza is here, guys," he informs me and Michael. We rush into the kitchen.

"Everyone, wash your hands!" Paula calls

out. That's just what happens at my house before dinner, too.

The pepperoni pizza is yummy and I start to take my second slice when I realize the slice I was going to grab is gone. I look around and see Dragon eating it while sitting on the island countertop.

Dragon notices me and looks cross. "You should have woken me up, Warren," he says. "It's a good thing my sense of smell is so refined and I came down in time. So far I've eaten a slice of the plain, the mushroom, and now the pepperoni. But I'm not sure which is my favorite." Dragon gobbles up the rest of the pepperoni slice before reaching over to grab another slice of each pizza. He piles them on top of each other and taken a huge bite. "Mmmm . . . smooshpilk. That means my favorite is the three-layered slice."

Nia looks around the table. "We ate a lot!" she proclaims. "Don't eat too much more, though. We still have dessert."

"Yay!" Addie shouts. "We only get dessert

'cause Warren is here. Can you sleep over every night?" she asks me. Dragon is still chewing, but he nods his head yes.

Everyone laughs at Addie's question. I laugh, too.

Nia and Jayden start to take out the ice cream and toppings while Michael and I help Paula put the leftover pizza slices away. Dragon probably thinks he's helping by licking leftover crumbs off the table, but I just hope Michael's moms clean it afterward.

Soon my stomach is stuffed from mint chocolate chip ice cream, whipped cream, and hot fudge. I don't think the night can get any better, until Michael and I sit down on the couch in the living room to watch a TV show.

"I usually have to agree to watch something Addie can watch, too, which means baby shows," Michael says, and rolls his eyes. "But since tonight is the sleepover, we get to choose!"

Dragon makes himself comfortable on the

couch in between me and Michael. "Any dragon cooking-contest shows? Dragon talk shows? Dragon gardening shows? Any of those will do."

Michael finds a show about spy kids who travel the world in a super-fast hot air balloon. Dragon agrees it's pretty funny but says it could use more fire-breathing animals.

My eyelids start to feel heavy and I stifle a yawn. Michael opens his mouth and lets out a full yawn.

"I think that's the signal to brush teeth and change into pajamas," Nia says as she pokes her head into the room.

"And I think we missed our chance at the secret second dessert," Michael sheepishly whispers to me.

"It's okay," I tell him. Luckily I see that Dragon's already fallen asleep. He would not be okay with missing a secret second dessert.

Michael and I quickly get ready for bed.

"Do you want a bedtime story?" Nia asks

after we finish brushing our teeth.

"*Mom!*" Michael wails, and hits his forehead with his hand. "I told you not to ask that when Warren's here!"

Nia grimaces. "Sorry, sweetie. I forgot."

"Ugh, Mom! No calling me 'sweetie.'"

This time Nia looks like she's trying not to laugh. "Of course, Michael. Sorry about that. Have a good sleep, boys. And don't stay up too late."

Michael pulls my pajama sleeve to lead me down the stairs. "I knew at least one of my moms would embarrass me," he says after Nia is out of sight.

"I bet my parents would do that, too, if you were sleeping over at my house." Michael smiles and nods in agreement.

We reach the basement where the tent is set up. Someone must have taken my sleeping bag because it's all laid out in the tent next to Michael's, with a pillow at the head of each.

"There's no way we needed my mom to read us a bedtime story," Michael says. He puts his legs in his sleeping bag and sits up halfway.

I yawn again. "I guess I am pretty tired."

"You can't sleep yet! We have our own stories to tell. Scary stories!"

11

The Scary Part

I think fast. Dragon is probably still sleeping upstairs on the couch. What can I do to stop the scary stories?

I force another yawn. "I'm too tired to think up any good ones," I say.

"Don't worry, I have plenty," Michael replies.

And he does. He has a story about a grizzly bear terrorizing campers. He has a story about aliens invading a suburban town, one just like Eddington, New Jersey, where we live. He even has a story about pandas turned into killer zombies.

Eventually, I hear Michael's voice start to

fade, and before the panda-zombies can find their first victim, I hear light snoring. Michael is asleep. I am not. I am very wide-awake.

I take a couple of breaths and hope I can fall asleep. But then I hear a creaking noise. Then there are thuds from upstairs. It could be people walking around, or it could be killer panda-zombies. I crawl out of my sleeping bag to see where I put my flashlight. Just as I grasp the handle, I see blasts of light from outside the window.

It could be the aliens invading Eddington! Michael is still sound asleep and I don't want to frighten him, so I turn on the flashlight and slowly make my way to the staircase. I should warn Michael's moms and my parents they're about to be attacked. Unless there's the small chance it's not actually aliens. Maybe I should peek outside to check first.

I push the basement door open and look both ways. The hallway is clear. I tiptoe down the hallway toward the front door. I know it'll get cold just to open the door a crack to see outside, so I put on my boots and jacket that I left in the coat closet.

I'm about to unlock the door when something barrels into me from behind and knocks me to the floor.

"Aaaaah!" I shout.

"Double aaaaah!" Dragon shouts.

"Get off me," I grumble.

Dragon pushes himself off the floor and offers a claw to help me stand up.

"Why were you walking around?" I say, trying to remember to keep my voice down.

"I had to go upstairs to get my wing covers from Michael's room," he explains. "Then I heard somebody walking around and thought you might have been the marshmallow thief."

"The what?"

"I checked all their kitchen cabinets and drawers earlier and there are no marshmallows. I figured a thief must have taken them. You were sneaking around, so I thought it must be you."

I sigh. "Dragon, did you ever think that some people, like Michael's family, don't have *any* marshmallows in their kitchen?"

"You mean they keep them in the bathroom? That's just odd."

I shake my head. "I'm not a marshmallow thief. I'm here to look outside quickly to make sure aliens aren't invading."

"Do you think *they* stole the marshmallows?"

I roll my eyes before turning the lock on the front door to open it. It looks normal outside until I see another flash of light. I shudder and quickly close the door.

"There's something out there," I say, and can hear the tremble in my voice.

"Let's go and demand our marshmallows back," Dragon replies, and pounds his fist. "I mean, Michael's marshmallows. Anyone's marshmallows."

"We can't do that! What if they have special powers? What if they want to hurt us?"

Dragon grabs me by my shoulders. "Are you going to face your fears or what? Marshmallows are at stake!" He reaches behind me to open the door and pushes me forward. "I told you before, don't worry. I'll be right behind you the whole time."

I don't have a chance to tell Dragon that doesn't make me feel better before I'm already out the door. My teeth begin chattering and I realize it's much colder at night.

Dragon never gets cold, so he has no problem pushing me toward the flashes of light.

"Stop pushing!" I shout to Dragon, but it doesn't matter. The flashes of light are getting closer to us. They're becoming brighter. I put up my hand to shield myself from the light when I hear my name.

"Warren! You came! With ... your dragon?"

"Alison?"

Alison smiles at me. She's dressed in her jacket and boots, too.

"The alien looks just like Alison," Dragon whispers to me.

"What are you—Wait, you were scared at the sleepover?" I ask her, suddenly remembering our deal.

Alison looks guilty. "Well, not exactly. I'm sorry if you thought I was."

"Then why'd you come out with the flashlight?"

"Because I'm having *such* a good time at the

sleepover and I wanted to tell you!" Alison is
smiling so brightly I almost can't be mad at her.
"All the girls are super nice, and we had a ton
of fun! We baked cookies, made slime, and oh,
don't go into your bed tomorrow until you check
the sheets."

"What?"

"And when they wanted to tell scary stories, I

told them I didn't want to and they didn't make fun of me or anything! They were fine with it. I know you were probably the one to ask Ellie to invite me, so I wanted to say thank you."

"They really didn't make fun of you?"

"Not at all. I think we became real friends."

"That's great, Alison," I say. "But you had to tell me this in the middle of a freezing night?"

Alison's face turns a little red, which is amazing considering how cold it is. "I also wanted to make sure you were having a good sleepover? You didn't get scared, did you?"

Dragon snorts. I ignore him.

"Maybe I did get a little scared . . ." Dragon snorts again. "But I think I'm okay now."

"Good," Alison says. "I guess I should get back inside before someone wakes up and wonders where I am."

"Yeah. Goodnight."

"'Night, Warren." Alison turns her flashlight toward my house and makes her way back inside.

I take another deep breath. "What a weird night," I say.

"I know," Dragon agrees. "Whatever happened to the second dessert?"

I begin walking back to Michael's front door and Dragon quickly follows. As soon as we get inside, I take off my boots and jacket. I'm about to put them back into the closet when a voice startles me.

"You scared me!"

12

Whizzaloomp

I turn around to see Michael looking at me with his hands on his hips. His glasses are back on. "Why were you outside?" he asks. "Are you okay? I woke up and you were gone. I was so scared. I almost told my moms you were missing. They'd never let me have a sleepover again!"

"I'm sorry," I tell him. "I'm really, really sorry. I saw a light from outside, and I thought it was aliens, so I went to check. It wasn't aliens. It wasn't anything bad."

"You thought it was aliens?" Michaels says, his eyebrows high.

"Well, it sounds silly when you say it aloud," I confess.

Michael giggles. "Maybe I shouldn't have told that alien story before bedtime."

"This is really embarrassing," I say.

Michael stops giggling and shakes his head. "Don't be embarrassed. I don't think it's as bad as my mom calling me 'sweetie.'"

"No, this is way worse," I reply with a grin.

"Even worse than Addie ruining our checkers game?"

"That was pretty bad," I say with a giggle of my own.

Dragon nudges me. "Michael is a real friend, you know?"

I think about it for a moment, and then take my final deep breath of the night. "But I can top that, Michael. The really embarrassing thing is that I didn't want to hear any scary stories. I was worried all week I'd get scared and want to go home tonight. But I didn't for almost all of it! I had so much fun all night! Until the scary stories. And I should've just told you I didn't want to hear them. I thought you'd think I was a baby."

Michael's quiet for a minute before he speaks. "I don't think there's anything wrong with not wanting to hear scary stories."

"You don't?" I say, surprised.

Michael shakes his head. "Of course not! I only told them because I wanted to impress you."

"Really?" I ask. I'm confused.

"Jayden told me when he was at overnight camp, all the older kids told scary stories at night. You're a little older than me, so I thought you'd think it was cool. Plus, the whole reason I invited you to *my* house for my first sleepover is because I've been too worried to sleep at someone else's house in case I miss my family. I thought you'd think *I* was weird if I admitted it."

Huh. That's not what I was expecting.

"That's not weird at all, Michael," I say.

Dragon yawns next to me. "This is really touching, fellas. But I've got to get in my beauty sleep before tomorrow. I'm quite scary looking without it." He passes by me to flop down on the couch in the living room.

"Want to sleep here instead of the basement?" Michael suggests, pointing to the couch. The couch is pretty big and has two sides connected like the letter *L*.

"Sure," I say, happy I won't have to try falling asleep in the basement again.

We bring our sleeping bags up to the den. Michael puts his on the empty side on the couch and climbs in. I scooch Dragon over as much as I can to put my sleeping bag next to him. Dragon gives a few snorts before turning on his side to sleep again.

I settle into my sleeping bag and realize that while I'm super tired, I'm not ready to fall asleep just yet.

Turns out Michael feels the same way. "I feel like we should tell a story before falling asleep," he says, "but not a scary one."

"Definitely not a scary one. How about a funny one?" I ask.

"Yes!" Michael agrees.

I think for a moment. "Okay, I've got it," I say. "Once there was a boy with a dragon, but no one else knew the dragon was really real."

"Ha!" Michael exclaims. "Like if your stuffed dragon was real."

"I'm real," Dragon murmurs in his sleep.

"Exactly," I say, and smile. "The thing about

this dragon is, he loves food. Like, really loves food."

"I like this dragon," Michael says.

"Me too," I say.

I finish the story and we eventually fall asleep. The next morning when I awake, I realize I wasn't scared at the end of the night. In fact, I'm feeling like I could go on a sleepover again sometime. I'm whizzaloomp. That means I'm happy. And also hungry.

"I smell bacon!" Dragon yells as he jumps up and down on the couch. "And pancakes! Woot! This is the best sleepover ever! Warren, schedule another sleepover for tonight and the next six hundred nights, okay?"

Dragon is whizzaloomp, too.